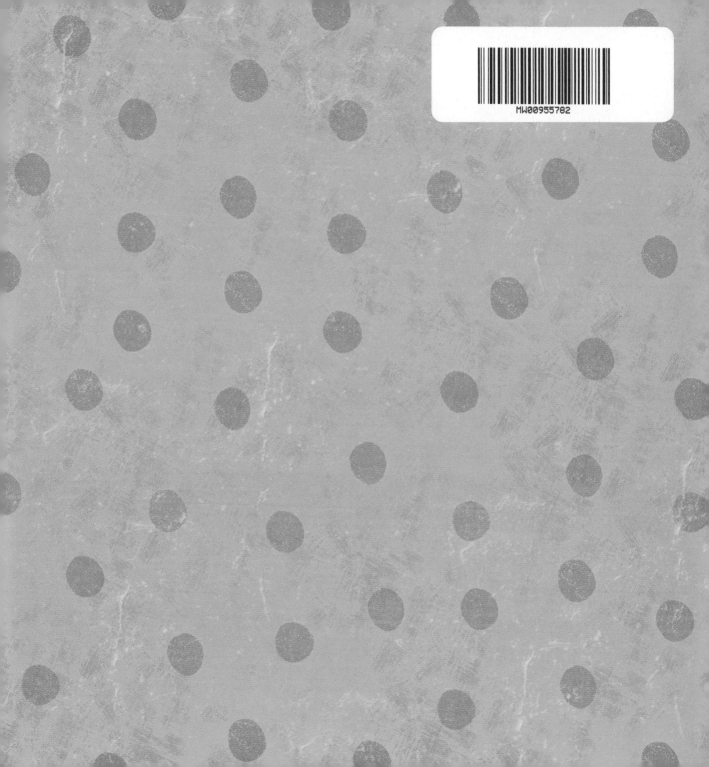

*This book is dedicated to each of you,
big and small, young and old,
turning the pages to discover how Allie
deals with an elephant on her chest!
My hope is for her actions to inspire
you to do the same.*

There's an Elephant on My Chest
Copyright © 2023 by Caris Snider
All rights reserved.

End Game Press books may be purchased in bulk at special discounts for sales promotion, corporate gifts, ministry, fund-raising, or educational purposes. Special editions can also be created to specifications. For details, contact Special Sales Dept., End Game Press, P.O. Box 206, Nesbit, MS 38651 or info@endgamepress.com.

Visit our website at www.endgamepress.com

Library of Congress Control Number: 2023930337
ISBN: 978-1-63797-067-6
eBook ISBN: 978-1-63797-077-5

Illustrated by Ana Sebastian
Design by TLC Book Design, TLCBookDesign.com

Printed in India / 10 9 8 7 6 5 4 3 2 1

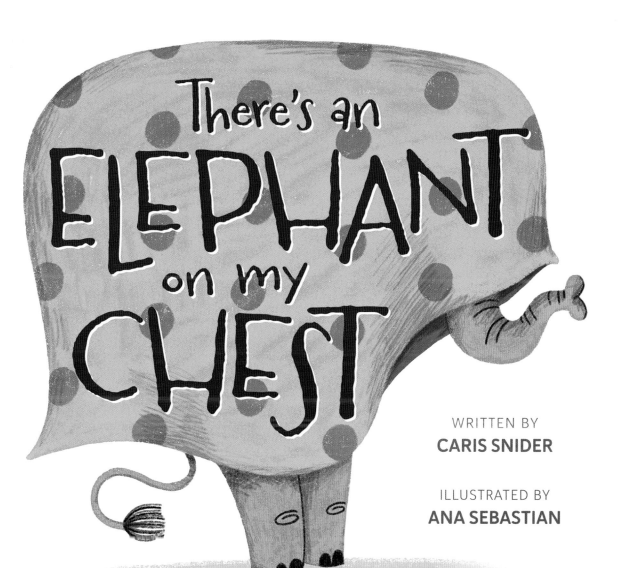

There's an
ELEPHANT
on my
CHEST

WRITTEN BY
CARIS SNIDER

ILLUSTRATED BY
ANA SEBASTIAN

"You, again!"

Why did you come back?!?

Allie pushed with all her might to the beating drum in her heart, but the weight was too heavy. There was an elephant sitting on her chest!

Frozen beneath a mammoth beast, Allie decided it was time to share her big secret. This elephant had been making frequent visits for a very long time, but this time, it felt even heavier.

"HELPPPPPPPP!" She screeched.

"There's an elephant on my chest!"

Her mom sprinted up the stairs,
puzzled by what she heard.
"Did I hear you say elephant?"

GULP... "Yes, an elephant."
With red cheeks and watery eyes, Allie whispered,
"I can't move it by myself."

"You are very brave to ask for help. Sometimes it feels scary, and you
may think you can't tell anyone. You did the right thing."

Knock! Knock!

Knock! Knock! Knock!

Allie's friends arrived to go to school. Gracie, Destiny, and Max bounded up the steps. They didn't see Allie's mom trying to stop them.

C-r-r-r-e-a-k...

It was too late. Allie's secret was out—she had an elephant on her chest—and now her best friends knew.

"It's okay, Allie," Gracie plopped down on the bed next to her. "Sometimes we have elephants, too."

Ruff! Ruff!

Allie glanced out the window to see Dr. Mike running behind Cooper for his daily walk. His fur sparkled in the sun while he chased his favorite tennis ball. "Dr. Mike! I need your help!"

Cooper pulled him into the house to see what was happening.

"Hello Allie...and elephant." Allie knew he could give her guidance to face the elephant on her chest.

"Try taking deep breaths instead of short, fast breaths to shrink the elephant. How about we all do it together!"

"Inhale...exhale... inhale...exhale..."

It worked! The elephant grew smaller!

The school counselor, Mrs. Miller, drove by, hearing loud cheers coming from the house. "What's going on up there?" she shouted.

"My elephant is finally shrinking!"

"HUH?" Mrs. Miller barely put her car in park before jumping out and heading for Allie's house. She had to see this for herself.

"An elephant has been on my chest, and we are working together to get it off."

Mrs. Miller could see gratitude dancing across
Allie's face when her feet landed on the top step.
She wanted to know what else made Allie feel grateful.

I am thankful for:

my bike

friends

family

glitter pencils

gummy bears

and my
fuzzy blanket...

**All of a sudden,
the elephant shrank**

smaller...

and smaller...

and smaller...

until...

I'm free!

Everyone applauded and celebrated!

"Yay, Allie! You conquered your elephant!" Sharing her secret, asking for help, taking deep breaths, and making a gratitude list gave her courage to face the day.

Allie waved goodbye to her Mom, Cooper, Dr. Mike, Mrs. Miller, and...the elephant.

Author's Note

Much like Allie, I had an elephant on my chest when I was her age. You see, I was born with a mild form of cerebral palsy in my left side. It caused me to hold my arm up and walk with a limp. A classmate made fun of me because this disability caused me to look different. I was crushed but told no one. I chose to hold it all inside. Every night when I would go to bed, my heart would race, my stomach hurt, and sleep was nowhere to be found. Thoughts raced through my head playing out worst-case-scenarios. I hid my heavy secret of an elephant until I was an adult.

I didn't know what I was experiencing was called anxiety. I discovered I wasn't the only one who dealt with this common and normal dilemma. When I speak at schools, I tell students anxiety is being overly nervous or afraid about what might happen, a reaction to a scary thought about a situation, or a response from a brain that thinks it is in danger.

When I finally asked for help, my elephant began to shrink as I learned how to respond. The coping skills, which are healthy ways to deal with anxiety, that Allie uses like acknowledging her elephant, deep breathing, talking to trusted adults, and gratitude, are just a few I still use today.

The goal of this book is to help you have courage and knowledge to face your elephant, right now. You no longer have to hide in fear or push it down. You are a brave generation, equipped with action steps to conquer your elephant!

Anxiety Symptoms

There are many symptoms children can experience when it comes to anxiety. The most common include:

- Rapid heart rate
- Irritability; anger
- Nightmares; unable to sleep
- Headaches
- Stomachaches
- Constantly being afraid or worried
- Social withdrawal
- Difficulty concentrating

For more information on anxiety symptoms, disorders, and when to seek professional help, go to: https://www.verywellmind.com.

Discussion Questions

- Who were the trusted adults helping Allie?
- Who else felt an elephant on their chest?
- How did Allie make the elephant shrink?
- Have you ever felt like you had an elephant on your chest?

Action for Your Elephant

- **Practice inhaling and exhaling** two to three times a day. Deep breathing keeps your brain from reacting in emotion so you can respond with clear thinking.

- **Write a daily Top Three Gratitude List.** Here is a link to a free printable to get you started: www.carissnider.com

- **The Senses Game.** For adults using this book to work with children, have them use their five senses to ground themselves back to where their feet are when thoughts want to carry them to a scary, faraway place. This practice offers a sense of calm and safety. Have a game time where they look for one thing they can see, one thing they can touch, one thing they can hear, one thing they can smell, and one thing they can taste. Have them yell out their answers. This is a fun way to help children learn how to use this coping skill to snap back into reality.

Caris Snider graduated from the University of Alabama with a Child Development degree. She has worked with children of all ages in and out of the classroom setting for twenty years. Caris travels the country speaking and encouraging adults and young people with her personal story of overcoming anxiety and depression. As a Certified Professional Life Coach, she desires to help people of all generations see their value, purpose, and worth through the eyes of God. She is the author of *Anxiety Elephants 31 Day Devotional* and *Anxiety Elephants 90 Day Devotional for Tween Boys & Girls*. For more information about Caris, go to: carissnider.com.